SECRET WEAPONS

A Tale of the Revolutionary War

by J. Gunderson
illustrated by Jesus Aburto

Librarian Reviewer
Laurie K. Holland
Media Specialist (National Board Certified), Edina, MN
MA in Elementary Education, Minnesota State University, Mankato

Reading Consultant
Elizabeth Stedem
Educator/Consultant, Colorado Springs, CO
MA in Elementary Education, University of Denver, CO

STONE ARCH BOOKS
www.stonearchbooks.com

Graphic Flash is published by Stone Arch Books,
A Capstone Imprint
1710 Roe Crest Drive
North Mankato, Minnesota 56003
www.capstonepub.com

Library of Congress Cataloging-in-Publication Data
Gunderson, Jessica.
   Secret Weapons: A Tale of the Revolutionary War / by J. Gunderson; illustrated
by Jesus Aburto.
   p. cm. — (Graphic Flash)
   ISBN 978-1-4342-0752-4 (library binding : alk. paper)
   ISBN 978-1-4342-0848-4 (pbk. : alk. paper)
   1. Graphic novels. [1. Graphic novels. 2. Concord, Battle of, Concord, Mass.,
1775—Fiction. 3. United States—History—Revolution, 1775–1783—Fiction.]
I. Aburto, Jesus, ill. II. Title.
PZ7.7.G86Se 2009
[Fic]—dc22   2008006251

Summary: The British are coming! Fourteen-year-old Daniel wants to join the
militia and fight against the redcoats. His father wants him to stay in Concord,
Massachusetts, and help run the blacksmith shop. Daniel thinks the job is pointless,
until he finds a secret stash of weapons in the shop's back room. Now, he must
protect the weapons from the British, or the American Revolution could be over
before it begins.

Art Director: Heather Kindseth
Graphic Designer: Brann Garvey

TABLE OF CONTENTS

Introducing 4

Chapter 1
Enemy in the Woods. 6

Chapter 2
Father's Secret 13

Chapter 3
Joining the Fight 18

Chapter 4
The Mission 26

Chapter 5
Rebel Blood 32

Chapter 6
Road to Victory 39

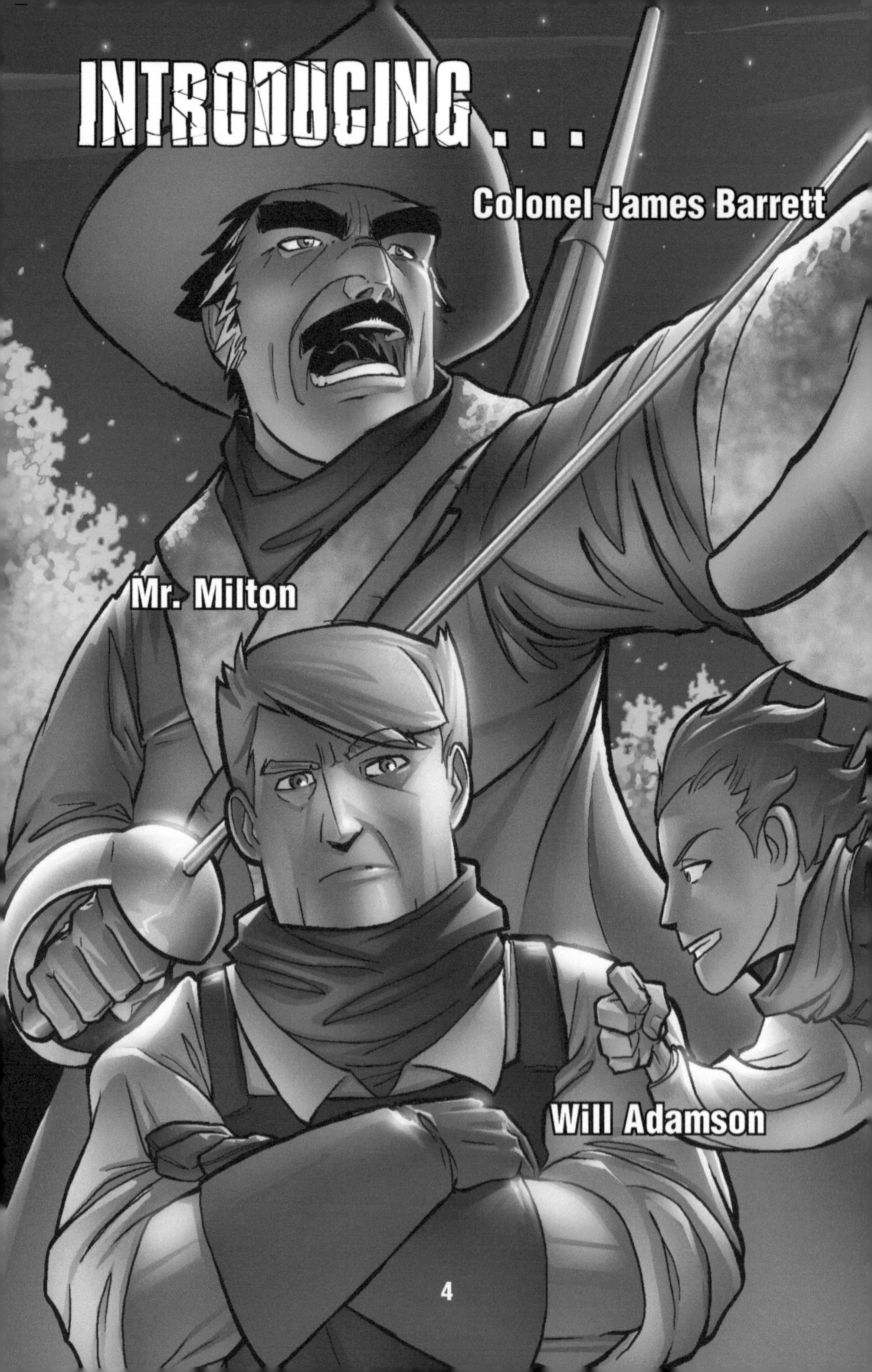
INTRODUCING . . .
Colonel James Barrett
Mr. Milton
Will Adamson

British Soldiers

Daniel Milton

Through the trees, I see a British redcoat! The enemy.

I crouch behind a tree, holding my musket tight.

I make no sound. I don't even breathe.

6

Chapter 1

ENEMY IN THE WOODS

Suddenly, I see another flash of red. I jump from behind the bush, musket in my hands, ready to face the enemy. I look around. Silence. The enemy is gone. Has he escaped? Maybe he's hiding behind the trees, waiting to attack. I grip my gun and turn in circles, searching for any sign of the redcoat. He is nowhere to be seen.

BANG!

The redcoat leaps from behind a bush, aiming his musket at my chest. I drop my gun, but it is too late. *BANG! BANG!*

"You got me good," I gasp, falling to the ground.

"Are you dead, rebel?" asks the redcoat.

"Not yet," I say. I scoop my gun from the ground and point it at him. "But you are!"

When I fire, he falls to the ground, moaning. Then he chuckles and sits up. "Nice one," he says. "I should've made you hand over your musket before I shot you."

"Remember that next time," I tell the redcoat as I leap to my feet.

The redcoat is really just my best friend, Will, wearing a red scarf around his neck. Our muskets are just toys, whittled out of wood. Today, he is pretending to be the British redcoat. I am the American militiaman.

"The British don't hide in trees," I tell Will. "They march in straight lines and don't even look around them."

"That's true," Will agrees. "But then it would be too easy for you."

"Yep! That's why, if war does break out, we'll have those redcoats whipped in no time!" I say.

War between America and Great Britain hasn't begun, not yet anyway. But the colonists won't keep letting the British raise our taxes and control our laws. War might be the only solution.

We crash through branches as we run toward Concord, where my father is waiting. Before we reach him, we drop the guns behind a mulberry bush.

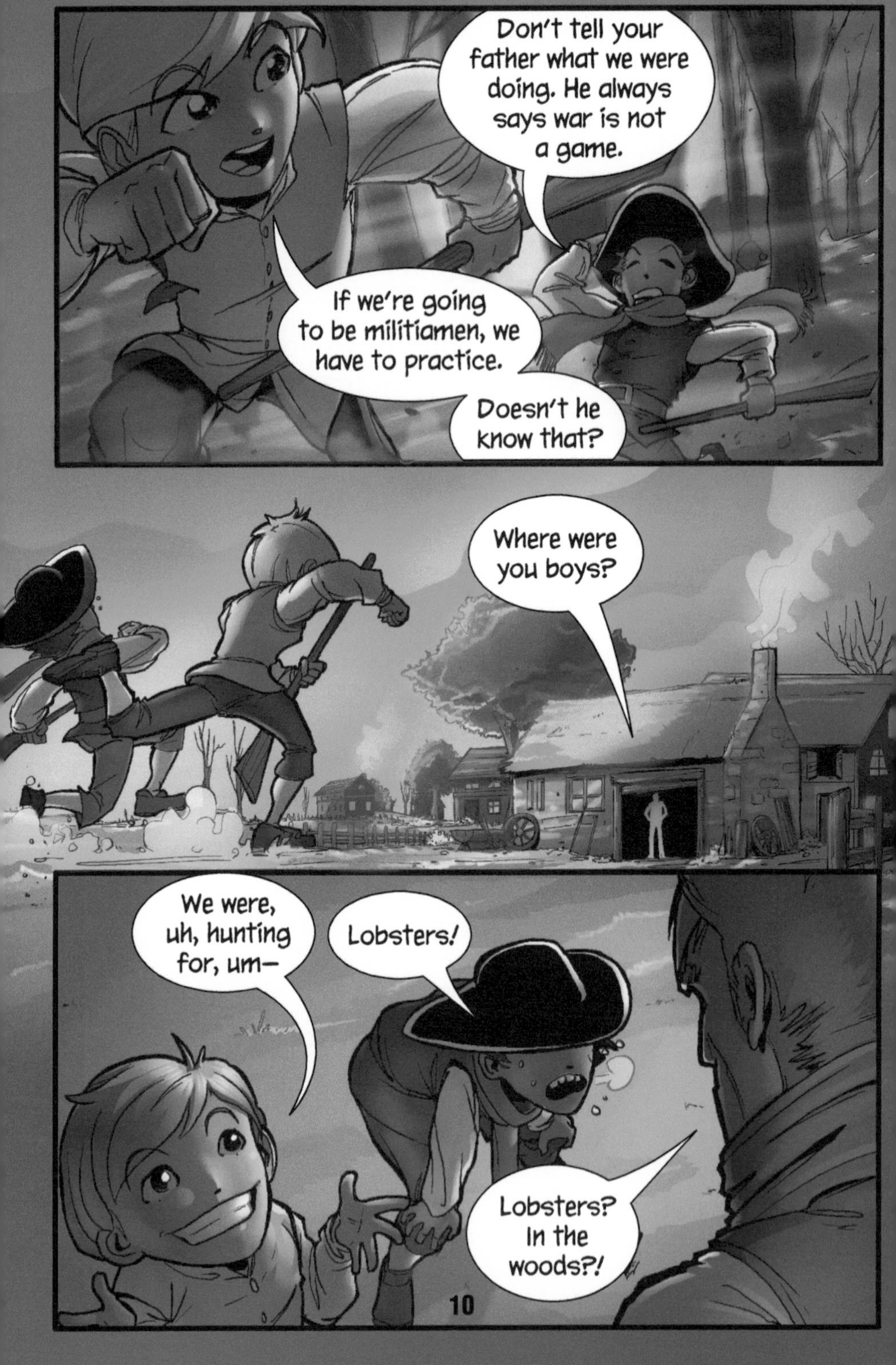
Don't tell your father what we were doing. He always says war is not a game.
If we're going to be militiamen, we have to practice.
Doesn't he know that?
Where were you boys?
We were, uh, hunting for, um–
Lobsters!
Lobsters? In the woods?!

Father's face reddens, but I don't know if it is from laughter or anger. "Come on," he says. "We have work to do."

Work, work, and more work. My father runs a blacksmith shop in Concord, and I am his apprentice. Most of my days are spent forging horseshoes and household tools over a hot flame. We are the biggest blacksmith shop in town and the busiest.

I scowl at Will and he shrugs, then heads toward his home. I follow my father to the shop. On the village green, the militia is gathered. The militiamen are local men. They are trained to be ready at a moment's notice in case of an attack by the British.

"Are you ever going to join them?" I ask my father. I already know the answer. He won't join them, and he'll never let me.

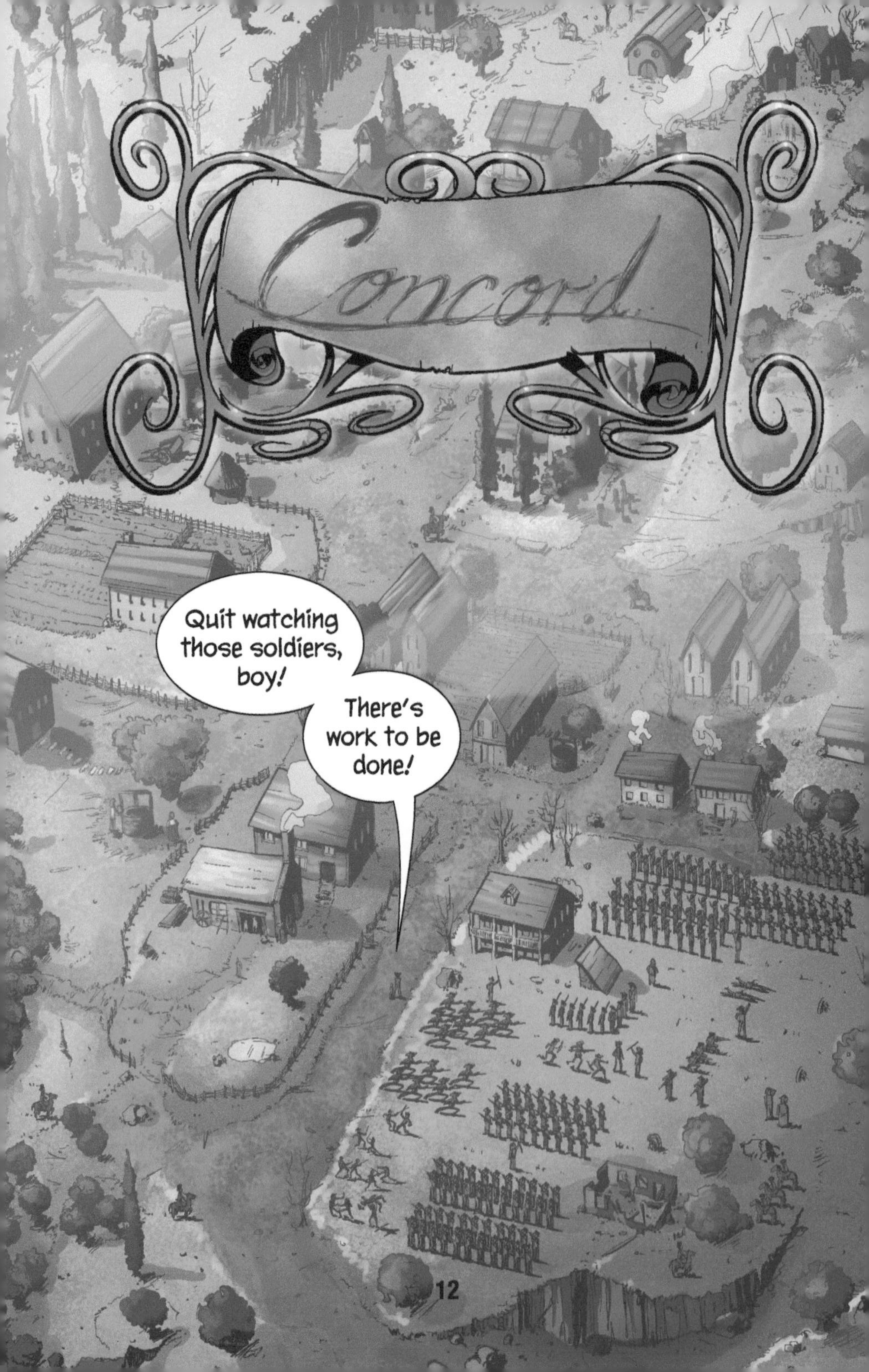
Concord
Quit watching those soldiers, boy!
There's work to be done!

Chapter 2

FATHER'S SECRET

Smoke rushes up my nose and into my lungs when I enter the blacksmith shop. Fire rages in the forge. I cough and wipe the sweat from my brow. It's so hot I feel as red as a lobster.

"We need five horseshoes, a fireplace rack, and a pot hook finished by the end of the week," Father tells me.

My mouth opens in surprise. The work is the same as this morning. Has my father done nothing all day?

"The tools won't forge themselves!" Father shouts. "Get to work!"

I turn to the forge and start working. I watch my father from the corner of my eye. He is bent over the forge in the back of the shop, working on something I can't see.

The fire in my forge is low, so I pump the bellows. The flames stand up like the fur on an angry cat's back. I hold iron bars over the forge until they are orange, hot, and ready to mold.

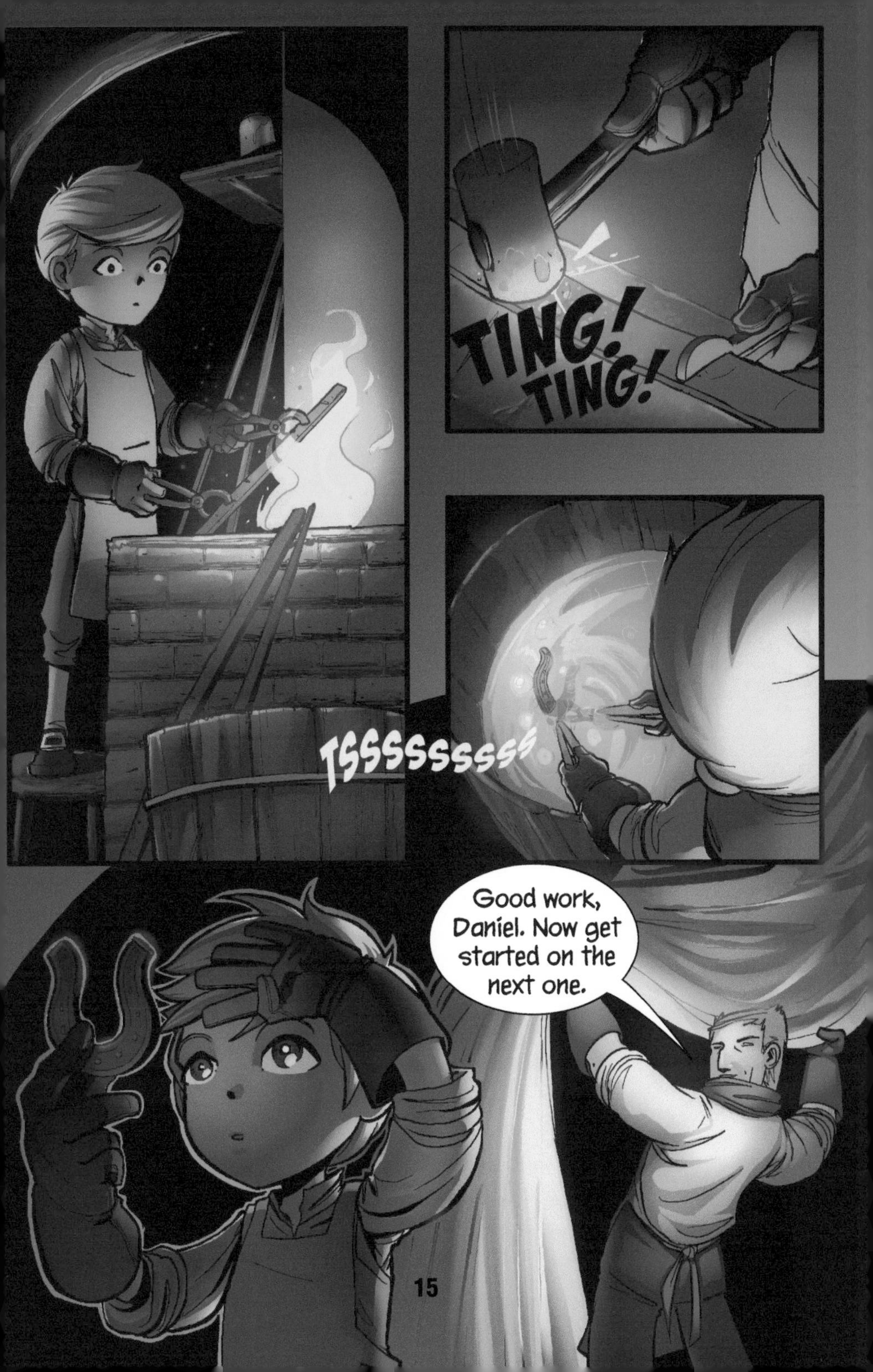
TING! TING!
TSSSSSSSSS
Good work, Daniel. Now get started on the next one.

As I get back to work, a man enters the shop. It's Colonel James Barrett, head of the Concord militia. I am surprised to see him here. Ever since my father refused to join the militia, he and the colonel aren't on good terms.

My father leads Colonel Barrett to the storage room at the back of the shop. When the door is closed behind them, I leave the horseshoes to cool and harden. Then I creep to the storage room door. My mind is spinning, and not just from the heat of the forge.

What is my father involved in? I wonder. It is not like him to keep secrets. *And what is behind the storage room door?* I can't hear a word, so I go back to work.

Soon, Colonel Barrett and my father exit the room. My father takes a key from his pocket and locks the door.

The storage room is never locked. There is something behind that door — something very important. Despite the heat, a cold chill shakes my bones.

Chapter 3

JOINING THE FIGHT

That night, I can't sleep. I toss and turn, thinking about my father and Colonel Barrett. I want to know what they are hiding in the locked storage room.

Father has always said that peaceful methods will solve the conflict between the colonies and the British. To him, rebels like Samuel Adams and John Hancock will only lead us to war. A war we won't win, Father says.

"Why then, is he suddenly friendly with the leader of the militia?" I ask myself.

The moon is high in the sky when I finally drift to sleep. I am asleep for only a moment when a sound startles me awake.

I sit up and listen. Outside, our neighbors are shouting. Hoofbeats shake the ground. Then someone pounds on the front door so hard I think it might break from its hinges.

The rider is gone, a dark, cloaked figure disappearing in the night. I run inside to wake Father.

"Father!" I call into the darkness.

My mother appears at the top of the stairs, holding a candle. "What is it?" she asks. She hadn't heard the warning.

"Tell Father to come downstairs!" I shout. "The British are coming! They'll be here any minute!"

Mother shakes her head. "It's just a bad dream, Daniel," she says. "Go back to bed."

I stare at her. "It's no dream!" I say. "Where is Father?"

From the look on her face, I know that Father is not in the house. I look out the window. Across the village green, the blacksmith shop glows with candlelight. I can see figures moving around inside.

I rush across the village green, wondering if it will soon become a battleground. The door to the blacksmith shop is shut. As I'm about to open it, I hear angry voices coming from inside. I quietly crack open the door and peek inside.

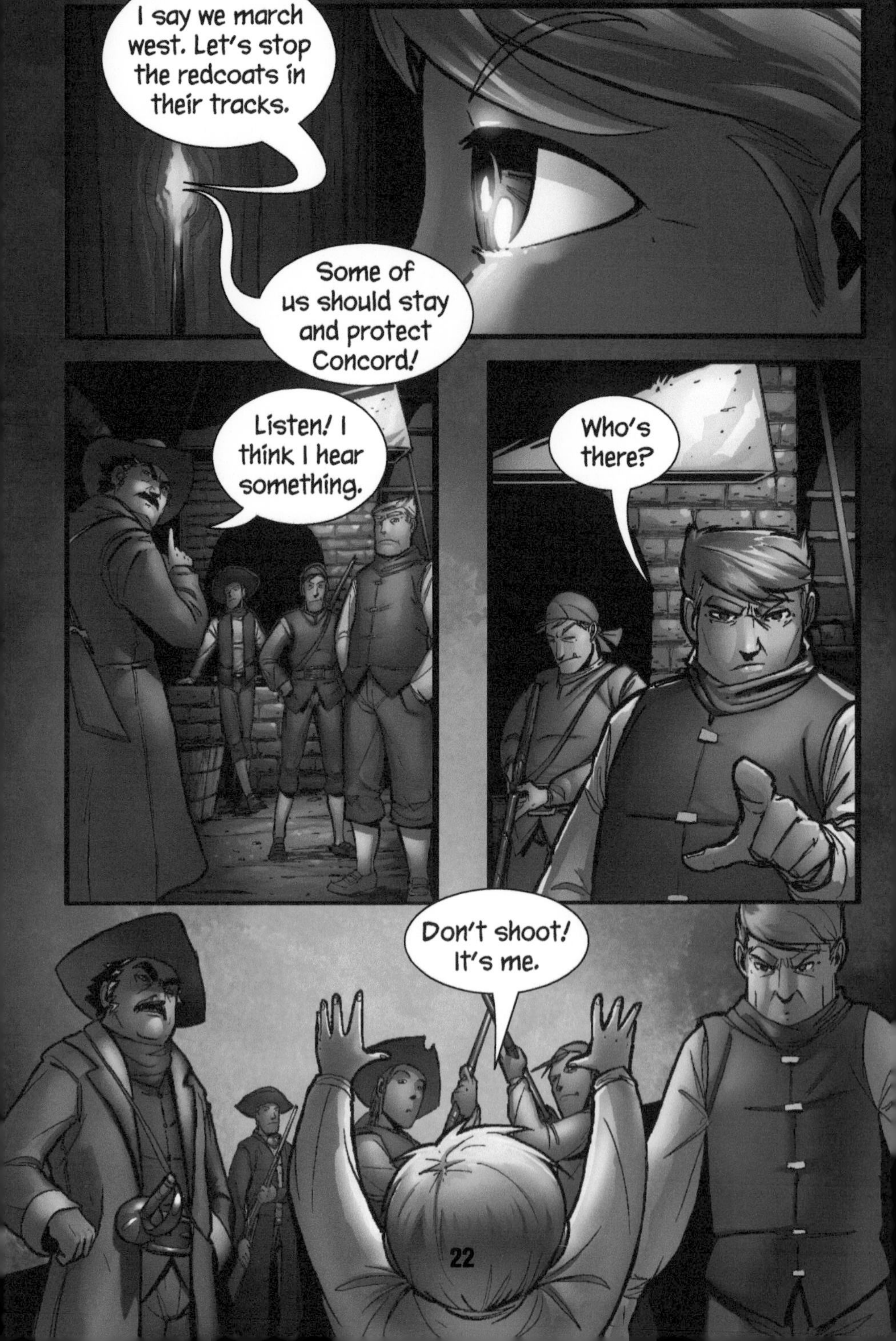
I say we march west. Let's stop the redcoats in their tracks.
Some of us should stay and protect Concord!
Listen! I think I hear something.
Who's there?
Don't shoot! It's me.

When I enter the shop, all eyes turn to me. I look at the faces of the men. Every last one of them is a militiaman.

"The British are coming!" I yell out.

The colonel laughs. "Thanks," he says. "But Paul Revere and Samuel Prescott beat you to it."

Father looks at me, crossing his arms over his chest. "Go home, Daniel," he says.

I don't want to leave. I want answers. Still, I don't want my father to be angry. I turn to go.

"Wait!" Colonel Barrett says, grasping my shoulder. His grip is so strong I cannot move, even if I wanted to.

"The boy could be of use," he says.

"I don't want Daniel involved," Father says.

Colonel Barrett doesn't listen. He puts both hands on my shoulders. I look him in the eyes.

"Do you believe the colonies should be free of British taxes?" Colonel Barrett asks me.

"I do, sir," I reply.

"Do you believe that the colonies should be represented in government?" he continues.

I quickly answer him again. "I do, sir."

"Are you willing to fight for the rights of the colonies?" he asks.

I glance at my father. He looks away.

"I believe we should use peaceful methods first, sir," I answer.

Colonel Barrett throws back his head and laughs. "You sound just like your father," he says. "But I must ask, what if these peaceful methods fail? Would you fight to defend your colony and your family?"

This time I do not look at my father. I know I will only see disappointment on his face.

"Daniel, do you know another trustworthy boy that can help carry out our plan?" Colonel Barrett asks.

I smile. "I know just the boy," I say.

Chapter 4

THE MISSION

Ping! Ping! Ping! I throw pebbles at Will's window, trying to wake him up. Suddenly, his shutters swing open, and Will looks out.

"Get dressed and come quickly!" I call softly.

"I'm too tired," Will moans, rubbing his eyes.

"Too tired for lobster hunting?" I ask. "Real lobster hunting!"

"I'll be down in a flash," Will says, grinning.

Will is full of questions as we walk toward the blacksmith shop. I can't answer any of them. All I know is that we're needed to carry out a secret mission. Colonel Barrett wouldn't tell me any more details.

The colonel greets us at the blacksmith shop. He scans the dark night, looking to see if we've been followed. Then he lets us in and fastens the lock behind us.

Your father and I would like to show you boys something.

CLICK!

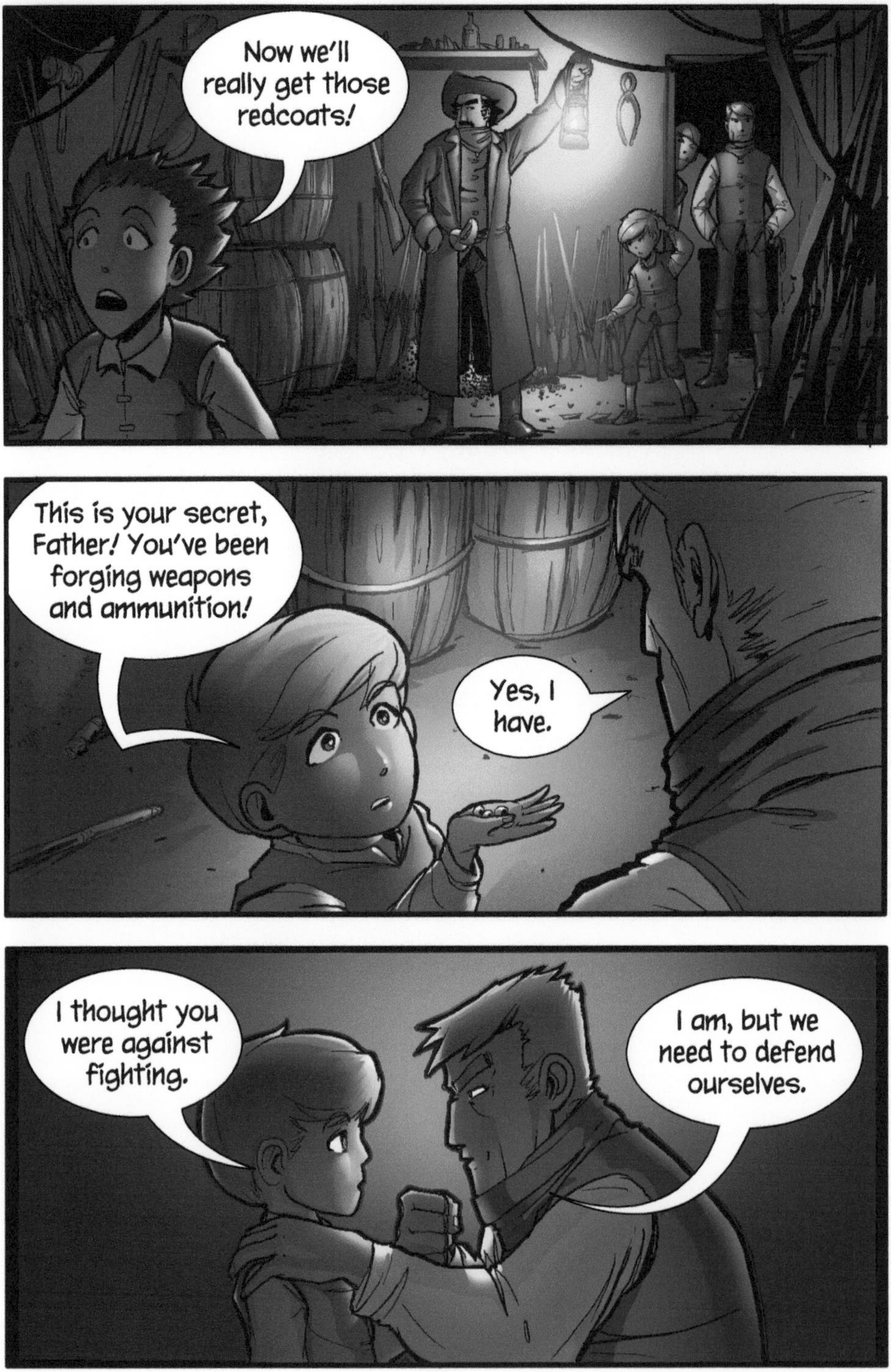
Now we'll really get those redcoats!
This is your secret, Father! You've been forging weapons and ammunition!
Yes, I have.
I thought you were against fighting.
I am, but we need to defend ourselves.

Colonel Barrett nods in agreement. "The King has ignored our requests for representation and freedom from the burden of taxes," he says.

I look at the weapons around me. "I have a feeling he'll listen to us now," I say.

"By the time we're through with them, those lobsterbacks will be swimming back to Great Britain!" Will shouts.

I lift a musket from the shelf. It is smooth and heavy, much heavier than my toy gun. My hands tremble. I can see myself already, lurking in the trees. I'll fire at any British soldier who dares enter Concord.

"Not so fast!" Father says, lifting the gun from my hands. "You won't be shooting anyone tonight."

"But I thought I was joining the mission!" I yell out.

"You are," Colonel Barrett says. "Just not in the way you think."

"The British found out about the weapons stored in Concord. They're on their way to take them from us," Father explains.

"We can't let them!" I gasp.

"Our militia is gathering to stop the British," Colonel Barrett says.

"We still need to hide the ammunition," Father adds. "That's where you boys come in."

"This is an important mission, boys," says the colonel. "Without your help, all of the militia's ammunition could be taken and destroyed. Our cause will be lost."

I think about the colonel's words. I wanted to be in the thick of the action. But the ammunition is important to the militia. Protecting it is just as important as the men behind the weapons.

"Good," Colonel Barrett says. "We don't have much time, so you must hurry."

My father hands me a musket. "This is for your protection," he says. "No matter what, do not fire unless fired upon."

As I hold the weapon, I secretly hope I do not have to use it.

Chapter 5

REBEL BLOOD

Later that evening, the Concord militia gathers beneath the stars. Will and I load the muskets, shells, and musket balls into a wagon. Will groans the entire time.

"All our practicing!" he grumbles. "All for nothing!" He peers at the militia on the village green.

"Keep working. The British could be here any minute," I remind him.

Finally, we finish loading the wagon. We pull the wagon into the woods. The bright moon above guides our way.

"Let's bury the ammunition and hide the guns under rocks and branches," I suggest.

We each grab an armload of ammunition and set off into the trees. We work quietly. We can't take a chance of being heard.

By dawn, we are almost finished hiding the ammunition and weapons. Bits of sunlight poke through the trees.

"I wonder what those British are up to," Will says, shading his eyes and peering toward Concord.

"There hasn't been a sound from the village," I say. "Do you suppose the Lexington militia sent them running before they even got to Concord?"

"I hope not! I want to see some action!" Will says.

I look around. The woods are still dark and shadowy in the sunrise. I shiver. "We'd better get back to work," I say.

I carry my last load deep into the thick of the trees. Will heads the other way. I cover the last of the muskets with some dead branches. Suddenly, I hear a sound that stops my breath.

The hoofbeats sound like thunder in the silent woods. It could be Colonel Barrett or my father coming to check on us. Then again, it could be British soldiers.

I walk softly toward the sound. As I get closer, I see a flash of red. This time, it is not just Will with a red scarf. It is two British soldiers, in flesh and blood.

I crouch low, barely breathing, trying not to make a sound.

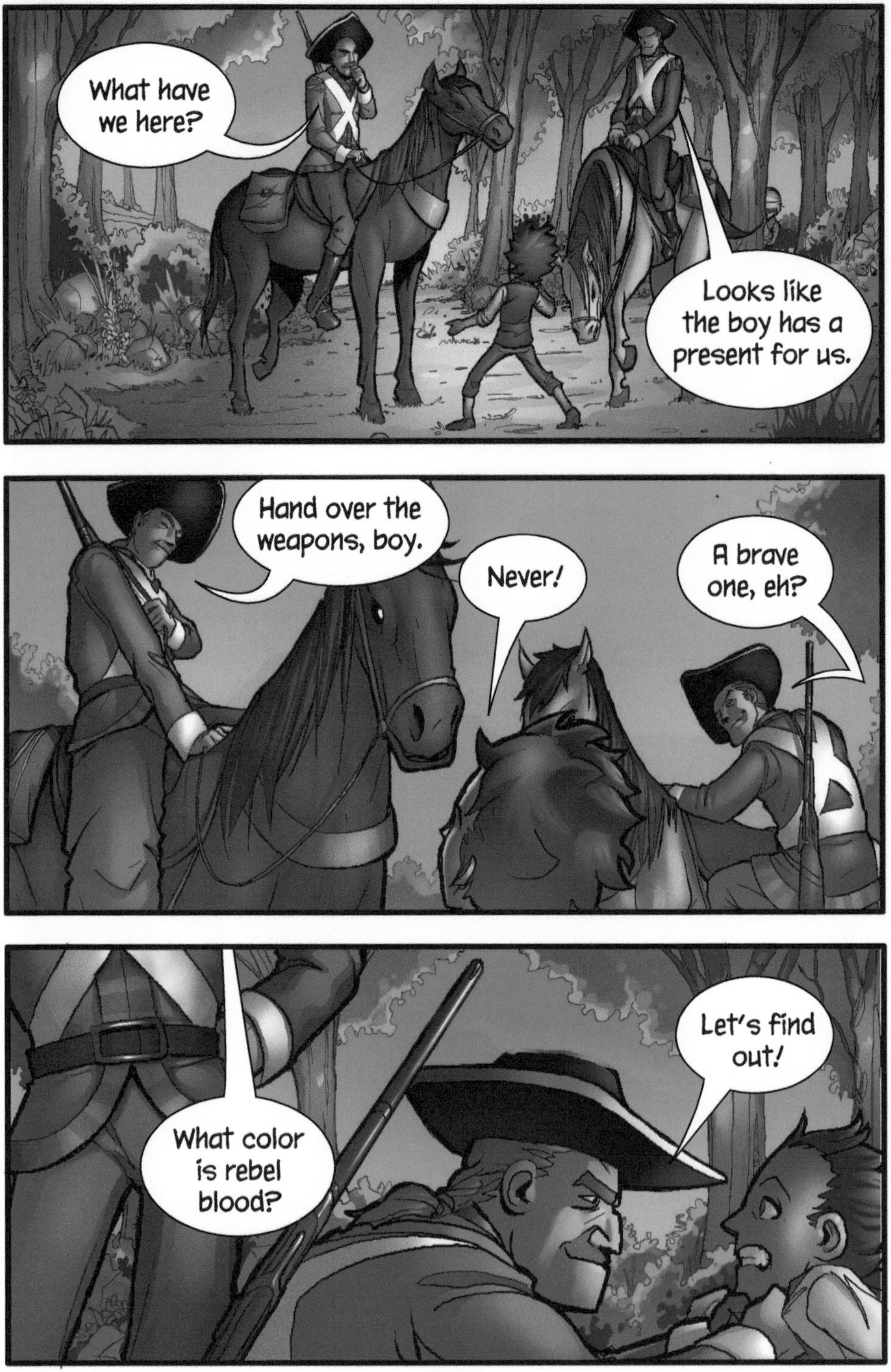
What have we here?
Looks like the boy has a present for us.
Hand over the weapons, boy.
Never!
A brave one, eh?
What color is rebel blood?
Let's find out!

Quickly, I grab my musket with sweaty palms. I remember my father's words. He always said not to fire unless fired upon. If I wait any longer, though, Will could get hurt.

Bang! I fire the gun into the air. The noise scares the soldiers' horses.

"Over here," I yell.

Will crouches down and grabs my musket. "Let's have lobster for dinner!" he says.

"Wait!" I close my fingers around his arm. "They're leaving."

The soldiers have turned and are galloping through the woods the same way they came. As they disappear into the trees, I hear a cry of warning. "We'll be back! Mark my words!"

When the last echo of horse hooves has faded, I leap to my feet. "Come on!" I shout. "We have to warn Colonel Barrett!"

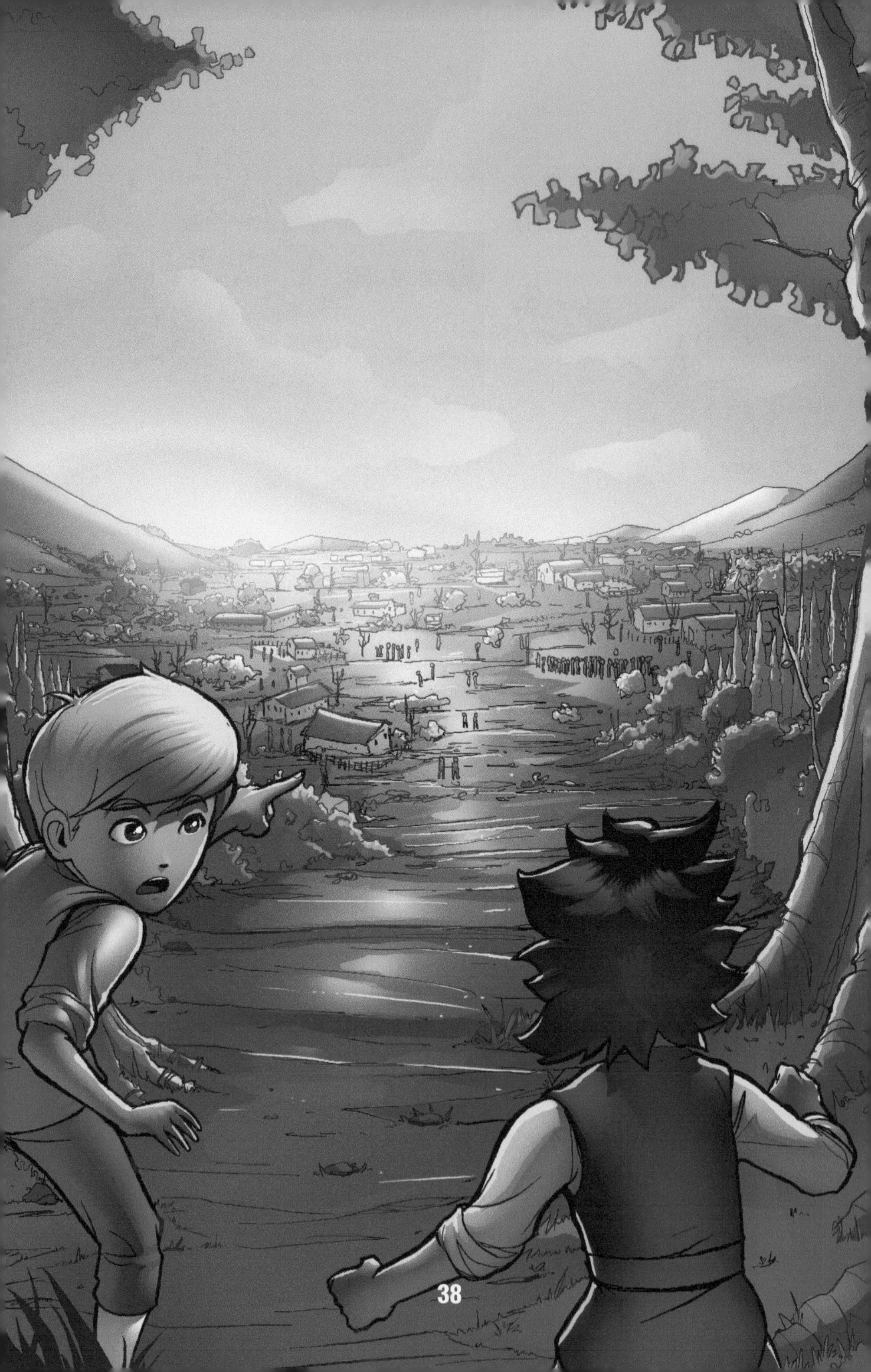

Chapter 6

ROAD TO VICTORY

The village of Concord is a sea of red. The militia is gathered on the green, facing the British soldiers.

Colonel Barrett sits high on his horse. "There has been a battle at Lexington!" he shouts to the crowd. "The Americans have lost."

A gasp rises from the colonists. They are shocked by news of the defeat.

"I now surrender the village of Concord," Barrett continues.

Will and I look at each other. How can Colonel Barrett do this? How can he give up so easily? Not even a single shot has been fired.

All around the village, British soldiers are flinging open doors of homes and shops. They search for the hidden ammunition. I know they won't find it here.

Will runs to check on his family. I head toward the blacksmith shop, hoping to find my father. The door hangs open. The British have already been inside! I peek into the shop.

"Mother!" I shout. She stands in front of the secret storage room, blocking the door. A British soldier points a musket at her. She must know what's in the room, or used to be.

The soldier sees me, but keeps his gun aimed at my mother. "Let the soldier in, Mother," I say.

"No! You don't understand!" she screams.

I stare hard at Mother, hoping she will be able to read my mind. She glances from me to the soldier and slowly moves away from the door.

Suddenly, I hear shouts coming from outside.
The British soldier glares at me and then rushes
out the door.

Outside, dozens of British soldiers are still searching the town's houses and businesses. Some of them have built a large bonfire in the middle of the street. They are burning all of the ammunition and weapons that they have found. A large cloud of smoke rises into the air.

The soldier from the blacksmith shop runs to join them. When he is gone, I hear a whisper come from behind the blacksmith shop. I slowly peek around the corner.

"Will!" I shout, glad to see my friend again.

"The militiamen haven't retreated, Daniel!" he says. "They're headed back over the North Bridge to save the town. Now's our chance to fight. Let's go!"

I take a last look at the blacksmith shop. My mother stands in the doorway. I know she'll guard it while I'm gone.

Soon, Will and I arrive at the North Bridge. Nearly a hundred redcoats are standing guard. Will and I watch as the militiamen approach. There's no way the British are going to let them through.

Ka-pow! A shot breaks the silence. I see smoke rising from the musket of a British soldier. Then suddenly, other soldiers begin firing, including the militiamen.

Captain Isaac Davis, the leader of the militia, is among the first hit. Other rebels have been shot as well. When the shooting stops, however, many of the British soldiers have fallen.

"Retreat!" yells the British colonel.

I look at Will. We both know the militia won't let them leave that easily.

We take a shortcut through the woods to the road that leads to Boston. Crouched behind a bush, we lay in wait for the British. Around us other militiamen are hiding. They don't pay any attention to us. Their eyes are fixed on the road. Soon, we see the bright red uniforms of the soldiers.

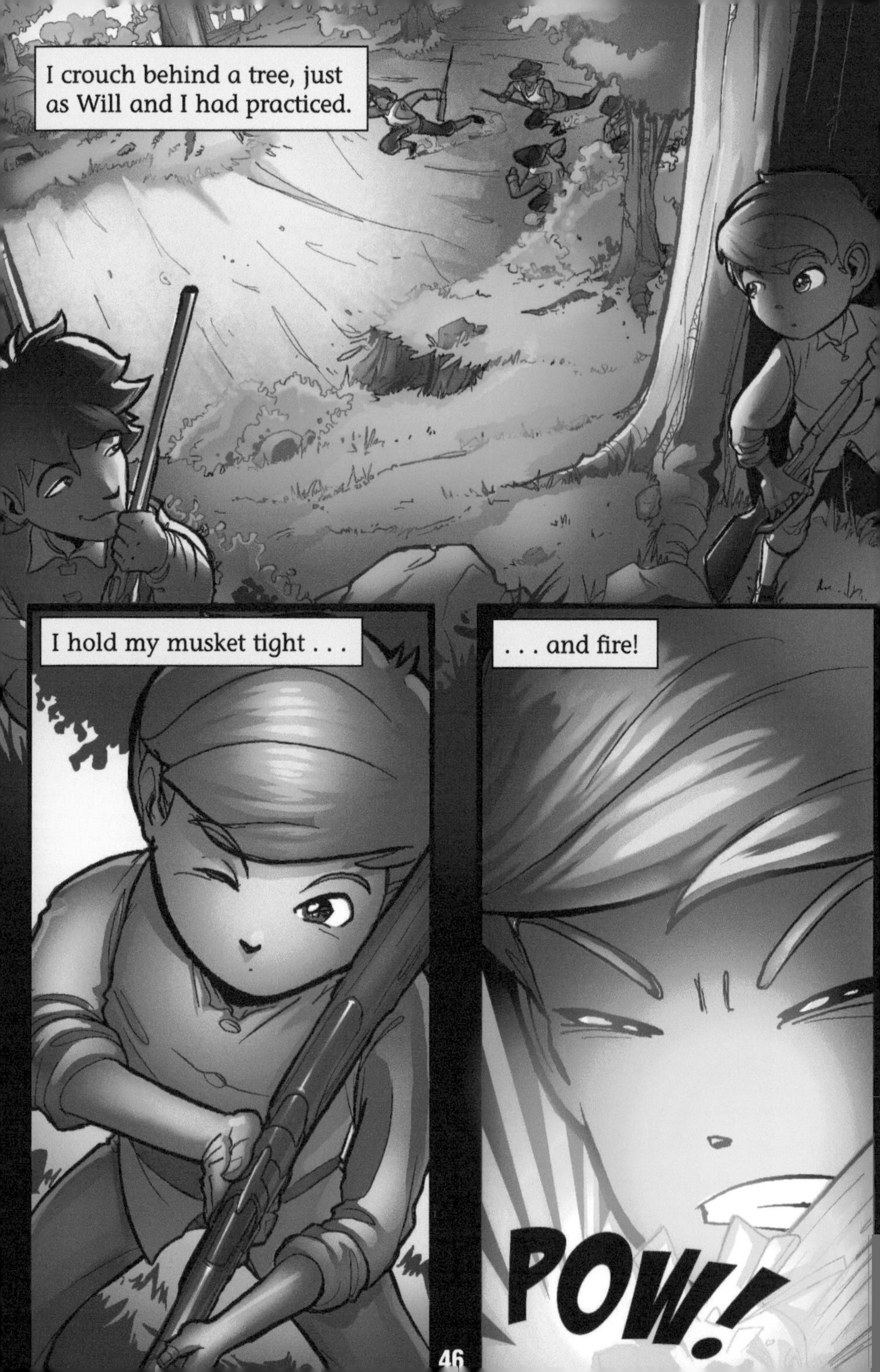
I crouch behind a tree, just as Will and I had practiced.
I hold my musket tight . . .
. . . and fire!
POW!

Smoke rises from my musket. The soldiers look confused as they fire into the trees. They can't see us, but we can see them. As I reload my musket, I hear a familiar voice.

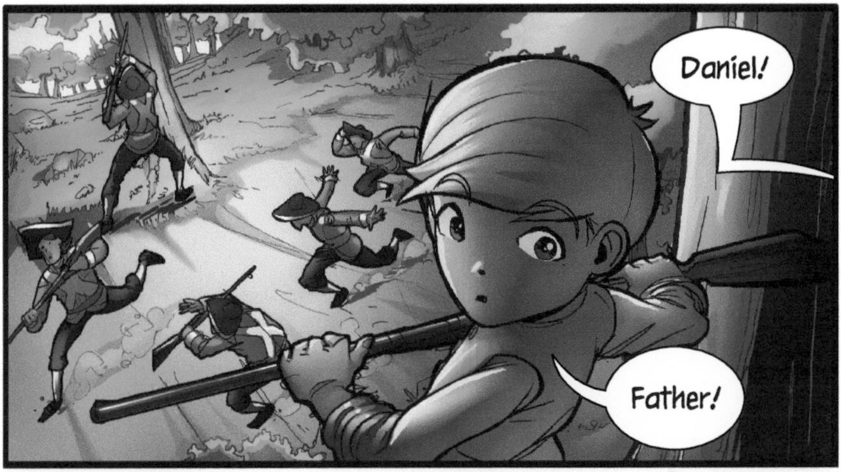
Daniel!
Father!

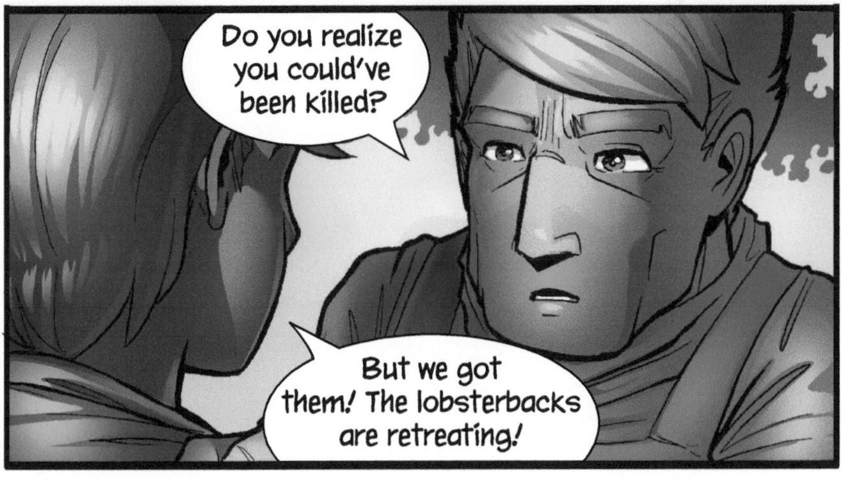
Do you realize you could've been killed?
But we got them! The lobsterbacks are retreating!

Father nods, but he looks worried. "We may have pushed the British back today, but I'm afraid they'll return in double force," he says.

As we walk toward the blacksmith shop, I take a deep breath.

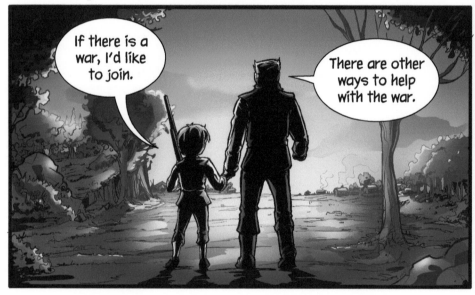

"I suppose I could make weapons for the militia," I say.

"Yes," he says. "You are needed here. If all the men are off fighting, the people of Concord will need brave young men like you to protect them."

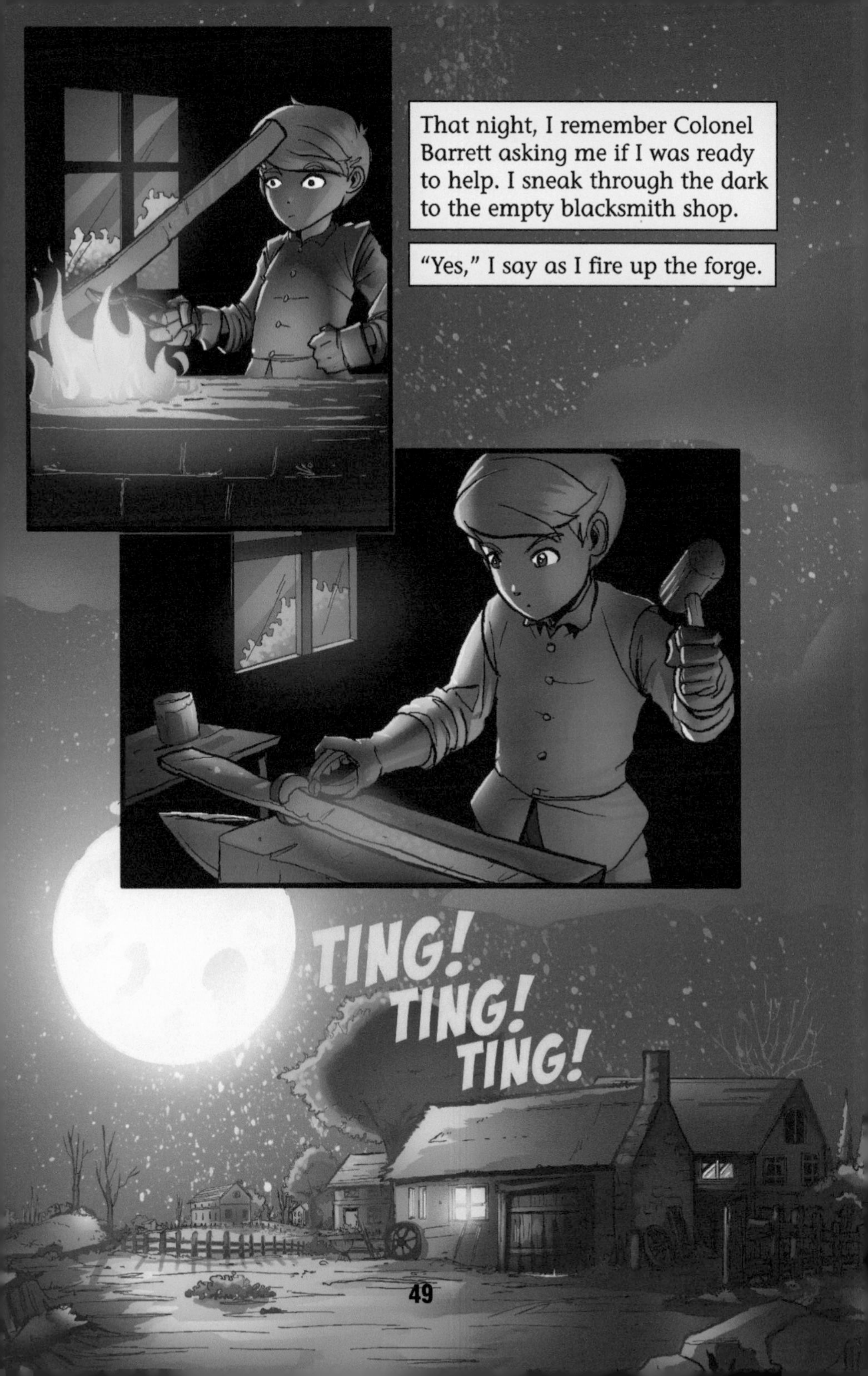

That night, I remember Colonel Barrett asking me if I was ready to help. I sneak through the dark to the empty blacksmith shop.
"Yes," I say as I fire up the forge.
TING!
TING!
TING!

ABOUT THE AUTHOR

Jessica Gunderson grew up in the small town of Washburn, North Dakota. She has a bachelor's degree from the University of North Dakota and a master's degree in creative writing from Minnesota State University, Mankato. She likes rainy days and thunderstorms. She also likes exploring haunted houses and playing *Mad Libs*. She teaches English in Madison, Wisconsin, where she lives with her cat, Yossarian.

ABOUT THE ILLUSTRATOR

Jesus Aburto was born in Monterrey, Mexico, in 1978. He has been a graphic designer, a colorist, and a freelance illustrator. Aburto has colored popular comic book characters for Marvel Comics and DC Comics, such as Wolverine, Ironman, Blade, and Nightwing. In 2008, Aburto joined Protobunker Studio, where he enjoys working as comic book illustrator.

GLOSSARY

ammunition (am-yuh-NISH-uhn)—bullets

bayonet (BAY-uh-net)—a long knife that is fastened to the end of a gun

bellows (BEL-ohz)—an instrument that is squeezed to pump air into a fire

blacksmith (BLAK-smith)—someone who makes and mends things made of iron

chaos (KAY-oss)—total confusion

colonies (KOL-uh-neez)—areas that are settled by people from another country and are controlled by that country

forge (FORJ)—a furnace that heats iron in a blacksmith shop

lobsterbacks (LOB-stur-baks)—a nickname given to British soldiers during the Revolutionary War because of their red uniforms

militia (muh-LISH-uh)—a group of citizens trained to fight in an emergency

musket (MUHSS-kit)—a gun with a long barrel that was used before the rifle was invented

MORE ABOUT THE BATTLE OF LEXINGTON AND CONCORD

During the late 1700s, Americans were growing tired of Great Britain's rule over the Thirteen Colonies. To protest British taxes, a group of colonists dumped a shipment of British tea into Boston Harbor on December 7, 1773. This event, known as the Boston Tea Party, angered the British government.

In the years that followed, tensions continued to rise. On April 18, 1775, Great Britain decided to stop any further colonial resistance. They ordered troops in Boston, Massachusetts, to march to the nearby town of Lexington. These troops planned to seize weapons from colonial soldiers called militiamen.

Fortunately, patriots Paul Revere and William Dawes discovered the plan. That night, they rode to Lexington to warn the town. When dawn broke on April 19, a day later known as Patriot's Day, the militiamen were ready.

PATRIOT'S DAY TIME LINE

4:30 a.m. — With the British a half-mile from Lexington, Captain John Parker prepares 77 militiamen for their arrival.

5:00 a.m. — Captain Parker's troops face off against British soldiers in a fight known as the Battle at Lexington Green. Eight militiamen are killed before the rest of them retreat.

7:00 a.m. — British soldiers arrive in Concord, searching the town for hidden weapons. Meanwhile, the militiamen regroup and wait.

9:00 a.m. — With 400 armed men, the militia rushes toward Concord. At the North Bridge into town, they meet a group of British soldiers. When the redcoats fire at them, the militiamen return fire, killing three British soldiers.

10:00 a.m. — British soldiers march back toward Boston. Along the way, they battle the militia, which grows to more than 4,000 men by the end of the day.

Months later on March 17, 1776, the militiamen, led by George Washington, force the British out of Boston. The American Revolution had begun.

DISCUSSION QUESTIONS

1. Mr. Milton hid the weapons he made from his son, Daniel. Why do you think he kept them a secret? Are secrets ever okay? Explain your answers.

2. On page 42, Daniel left his mother in the blacksmith shop to fight against the British. Do you think this was a good decision? Why or why not?

3. Do you think Daniel will continue working in the blacksmith shop with his father? Or, do you think Daniel will join the fight against the British? Explain.

WRITING PROMPTS

1. This story is known as historical fiction. The historical event is true, but the characters and story line are fiction. Choose your favorite historical event. Then make up a story that happens on that day.

2. In this story, the reader doesn't learn a lot about Daniel's best friend, Will. Write your own story about this character. Does he have brothers or sisters? What are his hobbies? Will he join the war against the British?

3. Many books and movies have a second part to the story. Write your own "part two" of this book. What will happen next?

INTERNET SITES

Do you want to know more about subjects related to this book? Or are you interested in learning about other topics? Then check out FactHound, a fun, easy way to find Internet sites.

Our investigative staff has already sniffed out great sites for you!

Here's how to use FactHound:

1. Visit *www.facthound.com*

2. Select your grade level.

3. To learn more about subjects related to this book, type in the book's ISBN number: 9781434207524.

4. Click the Fetch It button.

FactHound will fetch the best Internet sites for you.